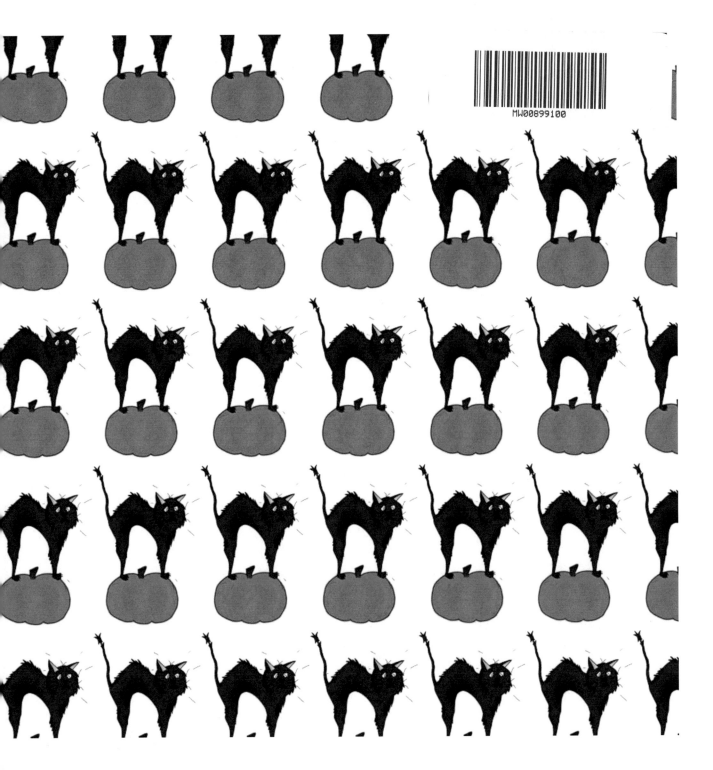

It is Halloween day, and all in town are preparing.

Everyone is excited to see what costume each will be wearing.

It is sure to be an evening filled with hauntingly fun festivity.

Everyone's Halloween decorations display so much creativity.

But this night brings no one else more thrill

than the old witch who lives at the top of the hill.

For on this day, she invites her friends to a party.

She cooks a big meal, so delicious and hearty.

The witch's house is old and creaky,

with the roof, faucets, and tub a bit leaky.

It is dark and lit only by candles in each room.

Finally, the witch tosses down her old broom,

she's dusted the furniture and swept the floors,

being careful not to disturb the webs hanging on the doors.

In her cauldron, she stirs her stinky green stew.

If you were to smell it, you'd say "Pee-yew!"

The witch throws in the final ingredient

and shoos away her cat,

who is quite disobedient.

She and her friends will enjoy the stew later for dinner,

but it's the pumpkin carving that'll make her party a winner.

She sets down the pumpkin

and goes to retrieve her knife,

when her mischievous cat hops up,

ready to cause strife.

With its little black paw,

the cat swats at the pumpkin on the table,

again and again,

until the whole thing is quite unstable.

"Shoo, you bad cat!"

scolds the old witch from the door.

But the pumpkin falls down

with a thump! on the floor,

and to her surprise,

it doesn't stop moving.

The witch cries "No!"

her voice loud and booming.

With the witch's house

so high on the hill,

the pumpkin picks up speed,

rolling even faster still.

The witch tries to catch up before it leaves her yard,

but she trips on an old rake that catches her off guard.

The pumpkin, still on the move,

tumbles through a graveyard.

And the witch huffs,

"Why, I've never run so hard!"

"Mrs. Bones," she cries,

"please stop that gourd!"

Mrs. Bones was

just sitting there bored,

so she reaches out to stop itwith her foot,

but that pumpkin will just not stay put!

"Ouch, my toe! I'm sorry, witch!"

Mrs. Bones cries out.

"Good luck catching it,"

she says with some doubt.

The pumpkin keeps on rolling, right past the graveyard gate,

heading for the swamp; she'll never catch it at this rate.

The pumpkin lands in the water, so murky and cold.

The witch won't enter the swamp, not even she is that bold.

"Can you grab it?" she pleads as her brows form a frown,

"I simply won't have time to get another in town."

The swamp's creatures

are all in a flurry,

swimming toward the pumpkin

in a great big hurry.

As they try to grasp it, they send water splashing,

but the pumpkin slips away amidst all the thrashing.

On the other side of the swamp,

the pumpkin finds dry ground.

But it doesn't stop there,

rolling into a cave without a sound.

At the cave's entrance, the witch calls out,

"Hello, is anyone there? Is my pumpkin about?"

But there is no answer.

So the witch, oh so brave,

tiptoes through the dark

and enters the cave.

She tries to be stealthy, fast but quiet,

for this is where bats like to sleep in private.

But soon she bumps her head

into something sharp and pointed.

"Ouch!" comes a voice from above,

 sounding rather disappointed.

Hanging from the ceiling of the cave is her good friend

Mr. Vampire. He says, "What is wrong, witch?

Your situation seems rather dire."

"I am in a hurry. Have you seen

my pumpkin?" the witch asks her friend.

Mr. Vampire quickly replies, "Why, yes,

actually, it just went past that bend."

Mr. Vampire turns his head and points to a curve in the cave.

"Oh, thank you!" shouts the witch as she dashes away with a wave.

Out of the cave, the witch is now deep in the forest.

She sits down, giving her feet a rest, as they are the sorest.

Surrounded by tall trees reaching into the sky,

the witch lets out a discouraged sigh.

Then from behind some bushes,

she hears a growl and a howl.

The witch cautiously approaches,

her face pinched in a scowl.

A dark figure is there, jumping up and down.

It's a werewolf holding his foot, with a large toothy frown.

"Oh, witch, was that your pumpkin that rolled over my paw?"

He points through an opening in the trees with a sharp claw.

"It was. I am so sorry!" she shouts as she continues to run,

wondering how this Halloween day lost all its fun.

The old witch is beginning to tire and slow,

says, "Oh, where did that silly pumpkin go?"

The witch finds herself in the middle of town,

with trick-or-treaters wandering all around.

She cannot see anything through the crowd,

so she drops to her knees and

calls for the pumpkin out loud.

The witch is about to give up all hope

and make her way

back up that steep slope.

When suddenly before her,

a small white ghost appears.

She sees a child draped in

white cloth as the crowd clears.

Then the sweetest voice

whispers in her ear,

"Excuse me, is this

your pumpkin right here?"

"Oh, thank you, dear child," the witch says as she stands,

rubbing her knees with her aching hands.

In the front window, the jack-o'-lantern is completed.

With everyone laughing, the whole party is seated.

Gathered together are the witch's friends she cares for most.

Including that sweet little trick-or-treater ghost.

All is good again on this Halloween night,

with everything now seeming to be alright.

That is, until the black cat wakes from his nap,

and spots the jack-o'-lantern, ready to give it a good whap!

THE END

This story is inspired by and dedicated to Landon.

Made in the USA
Columbia, SC
25 October 2024

45073304R00018